THE LATE BUS

RICK JASPER

NIGHT FALL

THE LATE BUS

RICK JASPER

MINNEAPOLIS

Darby Creek
A division of Lerner Publishing Group, Inc.
241 First Avenue North
Minneapolis, MN 55401 U.S.A.

Website address: www.lernerbooks.com

Cover photographs © Michelle McCarron/Photonica/Getty Images (bus);
© iStockphoto.com/appletat (silhouette).
Main body text set in Memento Regular 12/16.

Library of Congress Cataloging-in-Publication Data

Jasper, Rick, 1948–
The late bus / by Rick Jasper.
p.   cm. — (Night fall)
Summary: Bridgewater High junior Lamar Green begins having strange
visions of demonic figures preparing to attack the late bus, a route
recently taken over by the mysterious, disfigured Emmet Rumble.
ISBN 978-0-7613-7745-0 (lib. bdg. : alk. paper)
[1. Demonology—Fiction. 2. Bus drivers—Fiction. 3. Disfigured persons—
Fiction. 4. High schools—Fiction. 5. Schools—Fiction. 6. Horror stories.]
I. Title.
PZ7.J32Lat 2011
[Fic]—dc22   2011000962

Manufactured in the United States of America
1—BP—7/15/11

For Annie, always my
first reader

Deep into that darkness peering, long I stood there wondering, fearing,
Doubting, dreaming dreams no mortal ever dared to dream before

—*Edgar Allan Poe,* The Raven

I was almost seventeen, but it was my first funeral. Notso and I were all dressed up, standing in a crowd in the entryway of the West Bridgewater Baptist Church. Notso nudged me and rolled his eyes to the right. Coach Tyree stood there in a suit and tie, wearing a black armband and shaking hands with people like he knew everyone. We'd never seen him in his Sunday best before. I guess he and Miss Robin went to the same church.

"Are we supposed to sit down?" I whispered

to Notso. His grandmother died last spring, so I figured he knew the drill.

"Not yet," he whispered back and steered me into a line in the center aisle of the church. "When you get up there," he said, "just watch what everyone else does. I'll be right behind you."

By the time I was halfway up the aisle, I could see the casket with Miss Robin in it. A big woman. "A big woman with a big heart" is what people have been saying since she died, and I guess that's right. The kids on the Bridgewater High late bus, the regulars, always looked forward to seeing her. In fact, a lot of us attended this funeral, including the three I hung out with the most: Barry "Notso" Bright, who seemed to have detention more often than not; Nikki Presley, a reporter for the school paper; and Nigel Bronski, star of the BH chess team.

Miss Robin was the only bus driver who learned everyone's name. "Lamar, honey!" she'd say, grinning at me as I got on. "How was your day, sugar?" And if you wanted to tell her, she'd listen.

She passed away all of a sudden. On Christmas Eve. We were all been on break, but the school e-mailed everyone with the funeral information. No details about what happened, though.

And now I was about to look at a dead body for the first time. The lady in front of me walked up to the casket, looked in for a minute, bowed her head. Then she kissed her fingers, touched the body on the cheek, and moved on.

Miss Robin was wearing a white dress and a lot of makeup, and her hands were folded on her stomach. The casket was practically buried in flowers, and their smell was making me dizzy. Miss Robin looked like she was asleep. Trying to think of some words to say, I lowered my head.

Miss Robin's eyes snapped open. She looked around with a where-am-I? expression, then she saw me.

"Lamar! How you doin', baby?"

I was thinking that maybe I should be the one asking that question, but my throat was too dry. I couldn't say anything.

"That poor man! Lamar, you've got to help that man!"

My face must have shown how clueless I was.

"You'll know who he is, sugar. Just help him, promise?"

I heard myself stuttering, *"M-m-miss Robin? Aren't you . . .?"*

"Oh, I'm fine, honey. But that man needs you bad. Just . . ."

I felt a hand on my shoulder. It was Notso. "You OK, Lamar?" he whispered. I just nodded. When I looked down again, Miss Robin was asleep.

We sat pretty far back in the church. It was December, but the heat was amped and the place was crowded. Women were fanning themselves with the programs they got when they came in. When everyone was settled, Coach Tyree ushered some people to the front, where little velvet *Reserved* signs hung on the pews. They were Miss Robin's family, I guessed: a white-haired, very old lady in a wheelchair; a big man and woman who looked just like Miss Robin; and a lot of little kids.

It was a funeral, right? So I was expecting sad music, but the choir was all wound up. The piano pounded out "Glory! Hallelujah!," and people started rocking out. Some of them even got out into the aisle and danced. After the music came the preacher. He said nice things about Miss Robin—including that she was a big woman with a big heart. Every time he said a new thing, people shouted, "Amen!" And, in this moment, I noticed that I missed her, so I joined in here and there, even though I got funny looks from Notso.

At the end they sung some more, then they closed the casket. Six men in suits carried it out, followed by the family and a little girl, about nine, with long blonde hair and a brace on her leg. She limped along until she got to where we were. Then she turned for a second, stopped, and looked me right in the eye before she passed by.

I felt a chill, and I whispered to Notso, "What was *that* about?"

"What?" he said.

The church had a little graveyard where they buried Miss Robin. They lowered the casket into the ground, and people took turns grabbing handfuls of dirt and dropping them into the grave. It was cold, and everyone's breath was steaming. I dropped some dirt and Notso did too, and I was thinking it was all over when Miss Robin herself and the little blonde girl headed toward the casket. They both threw some earth, then looked over at me like they knew I could see them and no one else could.

I couldn't see their breath. The cold made my eyes water, and I wiped them with my hand. When I looked again, Miss Robin and the girl were gone.

I was shivering a little by the time the burial was over. I was trying to forget what I saw. I was just a little bit freaked out, maybe a little emotional. Like I said, it was my first funeral.

"Now the good part," Notso said. We followed everyone into the church basement. I don't remember ever seeing more food in one place before: a couple of big hams, dozens of casseroles and salads and cakes and pies, coolers of soda, and a big bowl of pink punch. There was a table in one corner where the family was sitting, and people lined up to sympathize with them. I recognized more than a dozen Bridgewater High kids and a couple of teachers.

I got in line. When I got to the family I shook hands with everyone and said, "I'm Lamar. Miss Robin was our bus driver."

The big man who looked like her suddenly started to pay attention. "Lamar Green?" he said.

"Yes, sir," I said, and he took me to one side.

"I'm Bill," he said, "Helen's brother. She lived with me and my wife and kids. She thought a lot of you, Lamar. She said you were a fine young man."

I was not sure what to say, so I asked, "What happened to her? I mean, how did she die?"

"She always had a bad heart," Bill said. "Even when she was a little girl we worried about losing her. She worked real hard Christmas Eve. Cooking and playing with the nieces and nephews, you know. Right after the kids went to bed she said she wasn't feeling too good." Bill's voice broke a little. "She said she was gonna lay down. An hour later we couldn't wake her."

I said I was sorry, even though it felt lame. Then Bill looked me in the eye. "Did Robin ever say anything to you about dreams?"

"No, sir. We talked a lot; my stop is the last one. But she never mentioned dreams." *In fact*, I thought with a little guilt, *she never talked about herself at all. Our conversations were always about me.*

Bill shook his head. "The last couple of weeks she was having these dreams. Said she couldn't remember much but screaming and fire. Then she'd wake up crying."

I couldn't imagine Miss Robin crying. "She always seemed really happy," I said.

"Well, she loved her work," Bill said. Then, "Thanks for coming, young man." He shook my hand again.

Before long I was sitting with Notso, and Bronski and Nikki were there, too. The three of us guys had piled our plates high. We all talked with our mouths full while Nikki picked at a salad.

"Why didn't you guys just bring a trough?" she said.

"Then we'd have to share," Bronski replied.

I asked no one in particular, "What do you think they'll do about the bus?" The late bus is for kids with after-school activities. It leaves at 4:30 and takes about an hour to get to the end of its route, out where I live. It's great, since a lot of kids don't have their own cars or parents who are free to pick them up. But we've heard lots of talk about the school cutting costs; the late bus is a luxury, blah blah blah.

"Well, it's already in the budget," Nikki said.

Since she was a reporter for the BHS *Beacon*, she knew something about everything that went on in the school. "So they'll probably just get a new driver."

We were quiet for a minute. I could feel our sadness over losing Miss Robin.

Bronski finally broke the silence, "You know, it's not going to be the same without her. Even on bad days, I'd hear, 'Hey, Bronski,' and, I don't know, it was like OK—bad day over."

This was too sentimental for Notso. "C'mon," he said, "it's just a new bus driver. What's the worst that can happen?"

The stuff that happened at the funeral wasn't completely new to me. Now and then, for as long as I can remember, I've seen things that other people don't. My dad says my mom—she died when I was a baby—was the same way.

I was, like, seven before I understood that some of the people I saw were dead. The first one I remember looked a lot like Dad, except he was younger and wore a soldier's uniform and had only one leg. When I told Dad his eyes got wide for a minute, then kind of sad.

"Well, Lamar," he said, "I guess you're seeing my older brother, Cletus. Got killed in Iraq a couple months after you were born."

At first I thought everyone could see dead people, but I learned that wasn't true. And I've figured out that it's usually a good idea not to talk about the things I see. Dad calls my visions a burden.

"Everyone is born with a burden and a gift," he says. "You've got to learn to live with the burden and use the gift." My gift, I guess, is that I'm good at sports.

Classes at Bridgewater High started again about a week after the funeral. At 4:15 on the first day back, the usual bunch of us were gathered in the foyer, waiting for the late bus: Notso, Nikki, Bronski, and me, Lamar Green, "jock in tights." I should explain the tag. My thing is sports. I lettered in football in the fall and baseball last spring. But most of the juniors at our school want to go to college, so we're running all over the place trying to do what our counselor Mr. Sprague calls "building our resume."

"Lamar," Mr. Sprague told me, "sports are good, but you're not the kind of elite athlete the colleges are going to come after with scholarships. And your grades, your SAT scores—they're average. You need another dimension. Like arts or community service or student government."

I needed, in other words, to build my resume. And right after our last football game, this girl Darcy told me how: ballet. I laughed really hard at first. I'm no dancer.

But she said, "You're strong and coordinated and we need some guys, Lamar. Please?" All right, Darcy was also hot. Anyway, I decided to try it, and it turned out not to be so hard. I thought of it like a sport with music, and it kept me in shape.

So there I was in the middle of winter in a letter jacket and tights, waiting for my ride home. When it pulled up we could see by the number it was the old, familiar bus. The driver was another story.

He wore a winter jacket zipped up to his neck, yellow work gloves, and a Red Sox baseball cap with the brim pulled down. But I noticed that stuff later. What none of could take our eyes off—no, that's wrong—what none

of us could keep our eyes *on* was his face. It had
almost no features, like a white mask with little
holes for eyes and a bigger one for a mouth. His
nose was a flat lump of scar tissue.

As kids got on the bus, a couple of the girls
put their hands to their mouths or made *oh-my-
god* eyes at each other. Some of us said hi as we
passed, but the driver just looked straight ahead
until everyone was on. Then he started on his
route.

The whole late-bus route took about an hour
one-way. I knew because my stop was last. This
time of year it was getting dark by the time we
left. Notso, Bronski, Nikki, and I didn't say much.
We just sort of looked at each other for a while
and then got into our books or our phones or our
music. Pretty much everyone else did the same.
The bus was a lot quieter than I'd ever seen it.

By the time the bus was mostly empty, I'd
moved to the front. When the last kid got off,
we were still about ten minutes from my stop,
traveling a winding, hilly road through the
woods.

OK, Lamar, I thought. *So his face is messed
up. Is that a reason not to talk to him?*

"Hey," I said finally, as friendly as I could. He didn't pay any attention. In the light around the driver's seat I could read a name tag on his jacket: *Emmett Rumble.*

"You a Red Sox fan?"

He still didn't say anything.

"My name's Lamar. Lamar Green."

He nodded his head at that, but he kept his eyes on the road. It wasn't like he was trying to be rude. It was more like he was watching the road for something, like he was expecting something. And the more I watched him, the more there was something familiar about him. I just couldn't pin it down.

It was obvious he wasn't much of a talker, though, and for a minute I started to miss Miss Robin pretty strong. Then suddenly we were coming up on my stop. As the bus slowed down, Emmett Rumble finally spoke.

"Here you go, Lamar."

His voice sounded like he had inhaled helium. It was high and tight, like a cartoon character's. I mumbled thanks and got down, and the bus sped off into the night.

I live with my dad and our dog, Marcus, down a gravel path about a hundred yards from the main road at the edge of the woods. The truck factory where Dad works is about as far away from home as my school, but in the other direction. A lot of nights we get home around the same time. I look forward to that time, when we get to find out about each other's days. And Dad seems to like it, too.

That night I told him about Rumble.

"Well, you did a good thing trying to talk

with him, Lamar," Dad said. "Face like that, he's prob'ly lonesome."

Since it was the first day after break, I didn't have a lot of homework yet. So after we washed the dishes, Dad and I watched a basketball game on TV, then turned in. I couldn't sleep, so I put on my iPod. Instead of music, though, I heard a familiar voice.

"How's it goin', Lamar?"

"Miss Robin?"

"Of course it's Miss Robin, honey. I ain't leavin' you all alone so fast."

"The new driver, Rumble? Is he the one you wanted me to help?"

"That's right. He's been through a lot, and he's got a lot to go through still. He'll need you, you'll see."

"Miss Robin, I didn't know you had a bad heart."

"Well, tellin' you about that wouldn't have helped. It just would've made you worry."

"Who was the little girl with you at the funeral?"

"My, you are full of questions tonight, Lamar. That's Penny. You'll find out more about her in good time."

"One more question?"

"Shoot, sugar."

"What's it like where you are?"

But the next voice I heard was not Miss Robin's. It was Rumble's.

"Here you go, Lamar."

"Here you go, Lamar."

And as he said, "Here you go, Lamar" for the third time, I heard other noises. Children screaming. Far away, a siren. And underneath it all, what sounded like a monkey house—an excited jabbering and squawking that got louder and louder until I yanked the earphones off.

I was sweating and my heart was racing out of control. I looked at the clock. I wanted to talk to someone, just to feel like I was back on Earth, but it was really late. What the hell—I tried texting Notso.

whats up?

It wasn't a minute before he was back to me.

whats up yourself? kinda la8 4 u.

cant sleep.

Darcy? lol

ha. I wish. bad dream.
bout?
our bus driver.
scary dude! thx for reminding me.

That's when I figured out what had bothered me about Rumble.

tty 2morrow?
yeah. I still owe detention from before Xmas.
HAHA. OK, Im gonna try 2 sleep again. ttyl!
Sweet dreams. lol

When dead people talk to me, I'm not usually all that scared. They can't really do anything but talk. Of course, sometimes that makes them mad, and they'll swear and cry and stomp around. But it's like a little kid's tantrum; it can't hurt me. The only scary thing about dead people is just that—they're dead. And I can feel that. It's not exactly a look or a smell. They just give off this vibe.

And that was the vibe I got from Rumble. Which was impossible, because he could do things; he could actually drive a bus. But everything else about him seemed dead.

The weirdness on the bus started slowly. The first week was quiet. At the end of the ride, I'd sit up front and say hi to Rumble, and he'd nod. He never acted like he wanted to talk, so I respected that. When he got to my stop, he'd always say the same thing in that wheezy voice: "Here you go, Lamar."

One thing did happen, though. We were about five minutes from my stop. Rumble was looking out at the road—kind of nervous, as usual—and two deer jumped out in front of us. It was dark and we were in the woods, so, pretty ordinary. But Rumble freaked out. He slammed on the brakes, even though the deer were pretty far ahead of us. Then he just sat there, sweating and breathing fast, staring into the woods like he expected a whole herd to surround us any minute.

Then he put his head in his hands, rubbed his forehead and his eyes, and sighed. Finally he started again, but for the next mile he drove really slow, looking back and forth into the woods on both sides. He even checked the rearview mirror over and over. When he dropped me off he didn't say anything.

The second week we made the school paper, thanks to Nikki:

Activity Bus Students Report
Strange Happenings

Last Monday, students on the 4:30 Activity Bus found their quiet ride interrupted by a series of unexplained noises.
"It was creepy," said Alice Herring, a sophomore and member of the girls'

basketball team. She was headed home after practice when the bus began to make noises that sounded "like a big animal growling, like a lion. At first I thought there was something the matter with the motor, but it got louder and louder." When asked how the driver reacted, Herring said, "He drove faster, like he was trying to get away from it."

Not all students on the bus, including the reporter of this story, heard noises. Students who did hear them agreed that they lasted about three minutes before ending abruptly. And strangely, while several students reported noises, none of their reports agreed on what the sounds were.

Ahmed Bell, a freshman Math Club member, said he heard "swearing and cursing. I thought it was someone on the bus, but everyone was looking around at everyone else, like 'What was that?'" Bell quoted what he heard, but the Beacon cannot print it.

Nigel Bronski, a junior on the chess team, agreed that there was a *disturbance. Bronski described high-pitched, earsplitting screams, "like you'd hear in a fake haunted house. I wasn't scared, but it gave me a headache."*

Haunting was mentioned by more than one student on the bus. The former driver, Helen Robin, died over winter break. The current driver had no comment. Coastal Transportation, the bus company serving BHS, did not return calls about the incident. Principal Weston said he had been informed about the incidents. "Whatever happened," he said, "and we are not sure anything happened, we're grateful that no one was harmed. Bridgewater High School values the safety and security of its students above all things."

I was on the bus that night and I didn't hear anything. I saw plenty, though. At first, some kids started to hold their ears and look around all wild. I thought the bus was filling with smoke. A gray haze seemed to thicken and settle on all of us. But then it began breaking up like a puzzle. The individual, smoky pieces took the shapes of shadowy, faceless people. For maybe a minute, while kids were holding their ears and freaking out, these creatures floated around the bus, as if they were exploring. Then they all seemed to get the same message, like a pack of wolves catching a scent, and they darted to the front of the bus and hovered around Rumble.

That was all. In just a few seconds the shadows merged and vanished. Then everyone started talking about the noise.

A few kids quit taking the bus. A couple even quit their after-school activities because they couldn't find a different ride home. At the same time, right after Nikki's story came out, a few thrill-seekers stayed late on purpose so they could ride what some were calling the "ghost bus." (And we, of course, were being called the "ghost bus-ers.") They got bored, though.

Nothing happened the rest of the week, unless you count the basketball game on Friday.

After-school groups don't usually meet on Fridays. Most students have other plans. And, during football and basketball seasons, there's usually a game that night. For away games, like the one that night against Cod Harbor, the activity bus usually joins a half dozen others to transport students to the game.

Sometime during the game that week, all four tires on Rumble's bus were slashed. Like the other drivers, Rumble had been hanging out in the parking lot, having a smoke. None of them saw anyone near the buses. After the game, kids found empty seats on the buses still available. As we drove away, I saw Rumble waiting for the tow truck, his cap pulled down low and his shoulders slumped. He seemed to be standing in the shadows. But as I looked closer, I saw that the shadows were alive, swirling slowly around him.

On Monday morning Principal Weston came over the PA with some words about vandalism. The school would pursue criminal charges if any BHS students were involved, he said. Bus service to the games would be canceled if this happened again, and so on.

The late bus showed up that afternoon with new tires. When we got on I said, "Hi, Mr. Rumble." I'd started doing that, whether he was going to talk to me or not. This time he actually looked at me for a minute, like he was searching my face for something. Then he turned away again.

We'd only been on the road for about five minutes when I started to see that gray smoke in the bus. No one else seemed to notice, but suddenly a girl in the back screamed. I'll let Nikki take the story from here:

Rodent Rage? Mice Attack Activity Bus

Screams filled the BHS Activity Bus Monday night as mice ran wild among the passengers. For almost five minutes, squealing rodents hopped from seat to seat, burrowing into backpacks and pant legs and leaping at students' faces. Some students stood in the aisles, slapping at the mice and screaming for driver Emmett

27

Rumble to stop the bus. Others opened the windows in hopes of encouraging the critters to leave.

"I had two mice in my hair!" sophomore Jenny Black said. "I tried shaking them out, but they were all over the bus. It was disgusting!"

Freshman Juan Arellano tried shooing the pests out the windows. But he reported that more mice came in the windows when he opened them.

Rumble seemed not to notice the commotion at first, but he finally pulled the bus to the side of the road and opened the door, at which point all the mice— some said hundreds—rushed outside and disappeared.

There were no injuries in the incident, although two students experienced allergy symptoms and another suffered a brief panic attack. The bus completed its route that night without any further disturbance. Principal Weston said the school would investigate. "It seems a little fantastic," he said. "Sometimes things *can get blown out of proportion. But we will learn the facts. At Bridgewater High School, student welfare is always our biggest concern."*

That's pretty much how it was. When the smoke came, the mice came. When the mice left, so did the smoke. As the ride wound down that evening, I sat up front by the driver as usual.

"That thing with the mice was pretty freaky, Mr. Rumble."

He nodded, but kept watching the road ahead.

"Seems like this bus is having some pretty bad luck lately."

He didn't say anything. We rode on through the night, darkness outside and awkward silence on the bus. It seemed like longer than usual before I could see our mailbox in the bus headlights. When we stopped Rumble said, "Here you go, Lamar," and I got down. I was turning up the gravel road when I heard his voice again, though, through the open door.

"Lamar."

"Yes, sir?"

"It's not the bus."

The door shut and he drove off. I suddenly felt cold, and it wasn't just the weather.

"What's going on, Lamar?" Principal Weston leaned across his desk and frowned. I'd been called to his office via the PA first thing that morning.

"Sir?"

"On the activity bus. Who brought the mouse?"

"Uh . . ."

"This hysteria is causing Bridgewater High a lot of problems, and it's only going to get worse if we don't get to the bottom of these pranks."

"Pranks?"

"Lamar, you're supposed to be some kind of leader on the late bus. So what's going on? After the so-called rodent attack, we found no sign whatsoever of mice. No hair, no droppings—you know you can't have mice without droppings—so this whole story seems kind of bogus.

"We—the administration—think this mouse incident is a hoax," he went on. "We think that someone brought a mouse on the bus and everyone freaked out. Did you see all the mice?"

"Yes, sir."

"Well, frankly, Lamar, I think you may have been caught up in the moment, all the screaming, just like everyone else."

Weston drew himself up. He was talking to me, but it felt like he was actually talking to a big audience.

"Lamar, Bridgewater High School has just about had it with these activity-bus incidents. It's only a matter of time before we're looking at lawsuits. It starts with a panic attack here, an allergic reaction there, and pretty soon everyone's jumping on the gravy train, trying to see how rich they can get off of our own Bridgewater High."

Suddenly he slammed his fist down on his desk. "It is *not* going to happen, Lamar! Not on my watch! I think you know what's going on. I can't make you tell me. But I can say this: if it keeps going on, the activity bus is finished. And maybe you and a few of your pranking friends are finished, too. Do you hear what I'm saying?!"

Has this happened to you? Somebody lays all this stuff on you all at once, so much stuff you can't even sort it out. And then they say, "Do you hear me?" And you want to say, "Yeah, I heard you, but this is so messed up I don't know what to say!" So you just say, "Yes."

Lunch found me sitting as usual with Notso, Bronski, and Nikki. I filled them in on my one-way chat with Weston. Bronski looked thoughtful. "So," he said, "what *is* going on with the bus?"

"Obvious, genius," Notso answered. "It's cursed. Haunted. Paranormalized."

"*Paranormalized?*" Bronski raised one eyebrow.

"The late bus," Notso intoned in a fake-spooky voice, "is a gateway to the supernatural."

"'Supernatural' is simply what people call things they haven't figured out yet," Bronski said.

Nikki weighed in, "Look, we know the mice thing wasn't a prank. The tire slashing . . ." She shrugged. "I voted for 'cursed.'"

"But why?" I asked. "We never had any trouble when Miss Robin was the driver."

"Why?" Notso said, "is the wrong question. The right question is: what can we do about it?"

Everyone was quiet. Finally Nikki said, "OK, this is going to sound weird, but when my family moved to Bridgewater, the first day we're in our house, one of the neighbors comes over and tells us the place is cursed."

"Wow!" Notso said. "And then it had *you* in it!"

"Cool it, Notso," I said, and turned to Nikki. "So *was* it?"

"The first week we'd hear noises at night. Nothing terrifying. And we all started noticing that sometimes stuff wouldn't be where we left it. Like the pillows on the sofa would be on the kitchen floor. Finally my Aunt Kate—she's a teacher at St. Philomena's—said we should get the house blessed."

Bronski rolled his eyes.

"Did you?" I asked.

"Yep. Aunt Kate brought a priest she knew, and he sprinkled the walls all over the house with holy water and said some prayers."

"And . . . ?"

"And the noises stopped. No more traveling furniture."

We all looked at each other. Finally Bronski said, "I don't expect it could hurt."

"Have a priest bless the bus? At a public school?" Notso howled with laughter. "I'm sure Weston would love to see *that* on the evening news!"

"Look," I said, "Thursday and Friday are half days for teacher meetings. The bus will be sitting in the lot at the bus company. That's just across town, close to St. Phil's."

I looked at Nikki, who was probably already thinking of the story she would write.

"I'll ask Aunt Kate," she said.

Three hours later I was in the dance room, doing an exercise called a *rond de jambe*. You support yourself on the bar and move your legs in a circle, front to back, back to front, to loosen up your hips. If you've never been in a dance room, it has bright lights and a special kind of mat on the floor. Horizontal bars hang along the wall for stretching and working on certain steps and positions. Three of the walls are covered with mirrors.

That day there were about a dozen of us dancers there, including Miss Kallas, our advisor. She's almost sixty, but she can do anything she asks us to do, and better. Someone said she had a real dance career in New York before she settled in Bridgewater. She told us we should learn to "feel" the positions first, then watch ourselves in the mirror. So I'd start by closing my eyes and, when I had the right feel, I'd look to check out my form. If there was anything out of place I'd adjust it, then close my eyes again and try to let my body remember how it felt.

That's what I was doing when I looked in the mirror and saw Miss Robin. She was holding the little blonde girl by the hand, and she looked serious.

"Hey, Lamar, how are you, honey?"

"OK. What about you?"

"Lamar, some stuff is gonna happen."

"The bus?"

"Yeah, that. Oh, this is Penny. Say hi to Lamar, baby." The girl nodded. *"But somethin' else, Lamar. It's about your daddy."*

"Yeah?"

"He's not well. He needs to rest. Will you talk to him about that?"

"Yes, ma'am."

"And the bus driver? You talked to him?"

"I tried, Miss Robin, but he's scared or something."

"Keep trying, Lamar. He needs you. Tell him Penny says thank you."

"What for, ma'am, he . . ."

"Lamar!" Miss Kallas's voice came from across the room. In the mirror there was just me. The other dancers were all lined up in front of her. "Having visions, Lamar?" she asked as I got into line.

When we were getting ready to leave, who

should come up to me but Darcy. "Was Miss Kallas right, Lamar?" she teased. "Were you seeing visions?"

"Nothing like the one I'm looking at right now," I said, smiling back. Darcy blushed, and I gave myself a mental high five. Sometimes I'm so cool I should be on TV. In fact, I was going to be on TV that very night.

Somebody had called one of the local TV stations about the late bus. When I joined my friends in the foyer, we could see the van with the dish on top parked outside. In front of the school office, someone was shooting video. A woman reporter who looked about my age was talking to Weston. He didn't look happy. Two guys in suits stood next to him. Later on I would learn that they were the owner of Coastal Transportation and a lawyer.

The bus pulled up right on time. As we tried to board, another reporter circulated through the group. A cameraman trailed behind her. Suddenly her hand was on my shoulder.

"Do you ride the activity bus, young man?"

I said yes, and she motioned to the camera guy to come in close.

"And your name?"

"Lamar Green."

"What year are you in school, Lamar?"

"Junior."

"In the last week there have been reports about strange happenings on the activity bus. Have you seen any of those?"

I thought about Weston's threats that morning. "Well, ma'am, I thought so. But some people don't agree."

"Lamar, do you think this bus is haunted?"

"No, ma'am."

Right about then Coach Tyree came out. He went to the bus and stood by the door as we got on.

"Students only," he said to the reporter when she and her camera friend tried to board.

"I need to interview the driver," she said. Coach shook his head.

"There's a schedule to keep, ma'am. You can talk to the owner of the bus company if you like. He's right inside the school."

When the doors finally closed and the bus
started on its way, everyone was buzzing
about the attention. I asked Nikki who she
thought might have called the TV station. She
looked shrewd. "I have no idea," she said, "but
I heard the family of one of the kids who got
allergic last week is suing the school district for
a million."

Notso grabbed his throat with both hands.
"I can't breathe!" he croaked. "Pay me!" Even
Bronski smiled.

The first part of the ride was uneventful. In due time I was alone on the bus with Rumble, with ten or so minutes to go until I was home. "Hey, how's it going?" I asked him. He shrugged and kept watching the road. I tried again.

"Did you know our old driver, Miss Robin?" He shook his head slowly.

I think I told you the thing about dead people talking. They don't always make sense. Sometimes what they say turns out to mean something later, and sometimes it never does. I decided to trust Miss Robin, though. I never had any reason not to when she was alive. So I said, "Penny says thank you."

Rumble swiveled toward me, and the wheel came with him. Suddenly we were swerving and skidding as he tried to stay out of a ditch. Finally he got control and brought the bus to a stop in the middle of the dark road. We were lucky no one was behind us.

Rumble was breathing fast. "What do you know about Penny?!"

"Not anything, really, Mr. Rumble. She's a little blonde girl, and I think she's . . . not alive. Sometimes I have . . . like, dreams. And my dream told me to tell you she said thanks."

The driver looked down at the floor. For a minute I thought he was going to talk to me. But all he said was, "She's got no reason to thank me." Then he got the bus going again. Before long I was standing by my mailbox, watching his taillights disappear into the night.

When I got inside, Dad was watching TV. "Hey, Lamar," he called. "C'mere! You're on the news."

Afterward he wanted to know all about the stuff that was happening, so I told him over supper. About an hour and a half later, I was in my room doing homework when he knocked on the door. "Come in," I said, and he did. And when I saw his face I felt my heart flip over.

You know the way you can live with someone but never really look at them close? Dad looked terrible. His face was dead pale, and I could see beads of sweat on his forehead. Dark circles lurked under his eyes.

I haven't told you much about Dad, except he works making trucks out in Fielding. I'm taller than he is, but he's in amazing shape at forty-something. Back in the day he was quite a jock. A couple of major-league baseball teams expressed some interest when he graduated high school, but his parents needed him around. "I was OK," he told me once, "but the majors . . . that prob'ly wasn't in the cards."

So he went to the factory and seven years later married my mom. Three years after that, he lost her and became a single dad. We've always been close. He likes to tell me about the time when I was a little kid, maybe in second grade, and we were talking about which one of us had known the other one for the longest time. Dad said we were the same, but I said it was me. "You've known me for seven years," I said, "but I've known you my whole life!"

When he came in looking bad, I jumped up from my chair and told him to sit down. He smiled a little. "It's OK, Lamar. I'm just tired. I was thinking I'd turn in early. I just wanted to . . ."

His eyes rolled up and he slumped over. I caught him and lowered him gently to the floor. I couldn't get him to come to. I dialed 911. They said an ambulance was on the way. All the time I was waiting I was thinking, *This can't happen.* I didn't dare to think about losing him.

The paramedics finally came. They hooked Dad up to some oxygen and wheeled him into the ambulance. "Can you drive?" one of them asked. I said sure and followed them in Dad's car to County Hospital.

The doctor found me in the waiting area about an hour later. "Lamar, right?" he said and shook my hand. "Your dad had a heart attack. He's stable now and he's resting, but we're going to keep him for a few days, run some tests to see if he needs any more procedures."

"Can I see him?"

"Sure, for just a minute. But then the best thing you can do is to go home and get some rest. We'll keep you up to date, and we'll call you if there's any change in his condition."

When I saw Dad he was sleeping. They had him hooked up to a monitor and an IV stand. I leaned down and told him I loved him and that I'd see him in the morning.

I tried to pay attention to my driving on the way home. That was easier in town, with the lights and at least a little traffic. But before long I was out in the country, where it was just dark.

Occasionally, I could see the lights of houses through the trees or a spotlight on a pole when I passed a farmyard. The moonlight made patches of snow seem to glow. I watched the white center line and tried to be alert for ice, but my mind kept leaving the road. I thought about Dad, going through the list of ways I couldn't help.

"Lamar."

Miss Robin's voice. At first I thought it was in my head, but I looked in the rearview mirror. There she was in the back seat, wearing the white dress she'd been buried in. She looked worried.

"How are you doin', Lamar?"

I started to answer and then—I guess it was just that someone asked and seemed to care, or maybe it was the long day—I couldn't talk. It took all my effort not to cry.

"I know, honey, you're worried about your daddy."

I just nodded. I was afraid to try my voice.

"He's resting right now, Lamar. But you'll need to be strong. Do you believe in evil?"

I didn't know.

"Evil is busy around here right now," Miss Robin went on. *"You can fight it, but you need to keep your eyes open."*

I managed a whisper. *"Is Rumble evil, Miss Robin?"*

"No, not that poor man," she said. *"But he's weary and weak. And evil follows him the way a wolf follows a blood trail."*

I slept that night the way you sleep when you have a fever: drifting for a little while, then waking up and remembering how bad you feel. In the morning I called the school and texted my friends about Dad.

Notso got back right away: *Sorry man. That's messed up. See u when?* I told him I'd be back in school the next day if Dad wasn't worse. Bronski texted me, and Coach too. Nikki was like *OMG call me!!!*

I was back down at the hospital at nine. Dad

was still in intensive care, but he was awake and talking, even though he still seemed tired. I did my best to hug him around the wires and tubes. Just like his regular self, he seemed worried about me.

"I'm sorry, Lamar," he said. His throat sounded really dry, so I helped him sip from a cup of ice by his bed. "That must have been pretty scary for you last night."

"It's OK, Dad. How're you feeling?"

"Not as bad as I look, prob'ly. Kinda surprised." He tried to smile. "I called the factory, and that's OK. I still have a job as soon as I'm back on my feet. Aren't you missing school?"

"Just today, Dad. I wanted to check in on you. Don't worry about anything. The house is fine, and I'm taking care of Marcus."

"I told the doc you were on TV last night. He said, 'I saw that! That was your son?'"

Just then the doctor came in and shook my hand. "I want to check on your dad," he said. "Wait a minute for me by the nurses' station." I squeezed Dad's hand and told him I'd visit him later in the day.

The doctor caught up with me a few minutes later. "Lamar, we're going to keep your dad a few more days. He's got two arteries in his heart that are significantly narrowed. We're going to do a procedure—not surgery—to open those arteries up. Then he'll need to take things slow for a while."

I was just grateful he was alive.

When I thought she would be at lunch, I called Nikki. "Lamar!" she said. "I thought you'd never call! Are you all right?"

I told her what was up with my dad and that I'd be back in school Thursday if nothing changed.

"That's great, Lamar," she said, then lowered her voice. "Look, I talked to my Aunt Kate. A priest from St. Phil's can meet us at the bus on Thursday at two."

"He said he'd bless the bus?"

"That's right."

"OK, cool. I have a car while Dad's in the hospital. We can drive over there from school."

The day went slow. I picked up around the house, worked some on a history paper that was due soon. Later in the afternoon I went back to the hospital. They'd moved Dad into a regular room, and we watched a little TV. It was dark by the time I was driving home.

When I pulled into the driveway, I noticed something missing right away. Usually, whenever Dad or I get home, Marcus comes out barking and jumping up on us. I called him, but he didn't seem to be anywhere around. Then something seemed to move in the corner of my eye, and something else flickered in front of me. I heard a faint sound, like when a bird flies near your head.

I walked kind of quick to the front door. As I unlocked it, I turned back to the yard. The hair on the back of my neck stood up. The clearing in front of the house was crowded with slithering shadows. They wound around each other like eels made of smoke, filling the gravel lane out to the road. They reminded me of the shadows I'd seen on the bus.

I hurried inside and locked the door. I thought of calling someone and felt lonely all of a sudden. No one knew that I saw things except Dad, and he never liked to talk about it, since it made him think of Mom. Anyway, he sure didn't need any more worry right now.

I'd forgotten about food. We had some lasagna in the freezer, so I put that in the oven. The package said *Family Size*. I sighed, realizing all this stuff with Dad was way getting to me. *OK, Lamar*, I thought, *get a hold of yourself.*

That's when I heard scratching at the back door. Marcus. But when I opened the door he wasn't there. And the yard was still swarming with shadows. Was it my imagination? I was sure I'd heard scratching. Then I noticed the door. From top to bottom, it looked like it had been attacked by a claw hammer; deep scratches and gouges crisscrossed the wood and splinters littered the back step. *Not Marcus.* I shut the door and set the deadbolt.

I turned on the TV just to have some voices in the house, but something was wrong with the reception. So I put on my iPod and tried to chill while I waited for supper to warm up. A minute later, though, I heard a noise that didn't seem to be part of the music, a kind of regular beat. There was someone at the front door.

I looked through the living-room window, but it was iced up, and anyway, it was too dark to see anything. Finally I unlocked the door and opened it.

Staring back at me was a white, hairless face twisted with scars: Rumble.

"I heard about your dad," he said. "I thought . . ." He held out a plastic grocery bag. I told him to come in. He had brought milk, bread and butter, eggs, and orange juice. Stuff I was glad to have. I said thanks.

"I'm heating up some lasagna," I said. "There's plenty." He nodded.

We sat down in the kitchen. Rumble took off his gloves and jacket. I could see that his hands were as scarred as his face. I wasn't sure how to start a conversation, or even if Rumble wanted that. But he spoke first.

"You said the other night. That you see things. Like dreams."

"Uh-huh."

"Are they always true?"

"I don't know. Sometimes. Sometimes they're just confusing."

"I have dreams. A lot lately."

"About what?"

"Wolves. Wolves chasing me."

"What happens? I mean, do they catch you?"

"Sometimes. And when they catch me, they turn into fire. I can feel the burning."

"But sometimes you get away?"

"Once in a while, when the wolves are just about to get me, someone chases them away." He paused a few seconds, then looked at me and said, "Penny."

"The little girl."

He nodded. "I know her. Can I trust you to keep a secret, Lamar?"

"Yes, sir."

He reached inside his shirt pocket, pulled out a folded piece of paper, and handed it to me. It was a small article clipped from the *Boston Globe*, dated about two years ago:

Fiery Crash Kills Two

Two people perished in a fiery bus crash in Dunport Tuesday night. Robert Emmett, 47, the driver of the bus, and Penny Abramowitz, 9, both died after the bus left the road, plunged off a cliff, and caught fire. According to survivors' reports, Emmett lost control of the bus on a patch of ice, causing it to veer toward the cliff, hitting several trees on the way. The bus came to rest on the edge of the cliff as its engine began to smoke. The driver unloaded 30 children through the rear door and jumped to safety before realizing that Abramowitz was still on the bus. Emmett went back for her. As he did so, the bus tipped over the edge of the cliff, falling some 75 feet and exploding in flames. By the time the fire was out, the wreckage and the remains of the two victims were incinerated, according to state troopers.

I handed the clipping back to Rumble. "You're Robert Emmett?"

"Yeah."

"How did you survive?"

"I don't know. I remember everything up to the crash, trying to get Penny, but then there's just a blank. I woke up the next day in my apartment. I had been dreaming about wolves."

"Didn't they look for you?"

"Everything was burnt to ashes. They assumed I was dead."

"Why didn't you tell them?"

"Guilt. I shouldn't have run off the road. I should have saved the girl. I just couldn't deal with it."

"What did you do?"

"I had some cash and a car. I headed out to California, got a new name, a new license. Driving is really all I know how to do."

"Why did you come back?"

"The dreams wouldn't stop. And when Penny started showing up in them, it was like she was calling me. I thought maybe if I came back, the dreams would go away."

We finished eating without saying anything.

"Mr. Rumble," I said finally. "Why did you decide to tell me about this?"

"What you said about Penny," he replied. "And these last few days, the dreams are different. When the wolves don't get me, when Penny shows up just in time, there's someone with her."

"Miss Robin?" I guessed.

"It's you, Lamar."

didn't know what to tell Rumble. I just said, "OK. If you figure out something I can do, let me know."

When he left, the shadows in the yard rushed after him. Like a pack of wolves, I thought. Then I heard a panting noise. Marcus came running up from wherever he'd been hiding in the woods.

Thursday morning I drove to school. On the way to homeroom I ran into Weston.

"How's your dad, Lamar?" he asked. I told

him, and he looked at his watch and said, "All right. Let me know if there's anything you need." I could tell he didn't care all that much. As he hurried off, I wondered if I'd sounded like that to Rumble.

Since it was only a half day, I met up with Nikki, Notso, and Bronski at 11:30. My having a car was a big deal for all of us, I guess. We drove to the Chowder Hut for lunch. Then they came with me to the hospital and waited while I checked in on Dad.

He was sitting up in bed. "They're gonna do this thing on Monday," he said, "where they blow up balloons in my veins to make them wider. Doc says I might feel better than I have in a long time." I was glad to see him in good spirits, and I told him I'd be back on Friday afternoon.

At ten to two we parked by the bus lot. Suddenly I realized we had a problem. The lot was several acres, and there were hundreds of buses parked there. How would we ever find ours?

"No worries," Nikki said. "They have numbered parking spaces. Don't you know the number of the late bus?"

Notso broke in. "Six-six-six?"

Bronski raised his hand. "Call on me, teacher!"

"Yes, Mr. Bronski?" Nikki replied.

"The activity bus is number 0331, license plate CT910331, since Coastal Transportation registered it in 2002."

While Bronski was showing off, a very tall, thin, robed figure was approaching from the direction of St. Philomena's. He carried a small black bag.

"Hi, Father Mark," Nikki called when he got close to us. He wasn't old, maybe thirty, but his hair and beard were streaked with gray. He had lots of lines around his eyes. His robe was brown, with a hood; he had a cord for a belt, and even though it was chilly, he wore sandals over his black socks.

"Are you Kate's niece?" he asked Nikki, then gave her a big hug. "My goodness, you're not a little girl anymore!"

Nikki blushed and introduced us—his name was Father Mark Mulroney—and we went looking for the bus. There was a chain-link fence all around the bus lot, but the gate near the office building was open. We walked through and started towards the buses. Then we heard a door slam.

"Hey, you kids, where do you think you're going?" The security guard caught up with us and looked us over. "This is private property," he said. "See the sign? *Authorized personnel only.* You'll have to leave."

While I was wondering what to do, Father Mark said, "Mike! How are ye t'day?" and held out his hand.

"Father Mark," the guard replied. "You know these kids?"

"Sure do. This is Nikki—she's Miss Kate Presley's niece. Nikki, Mike has twin sons in your aunt's honors class."

The priest introduced the rest of us. The guard was more relaxed, but still suspicious. "This some kind of field trip?" he asked.

"Nikki and her friends go to Bridgewater High," Father Mark said. "But she's a good Catholic girl, and she asked me if I'd bless her school bus. Isn't that something?"

"That's great, Father, but I'm not supposed to . . ."

"Ten minutes tops, Mike. It'll give young Nikki peace of mind. Nikki, which bus are we looking for?"

"Zero-three-three-one, Father."

The guard sighed. "OK. Go seven rows down and take a right. It's about ten buses in, on your left. Ten minutes."

"Bless you, Mike," the priest said, beaming, and we went on our way.

When we found the bus, Father Mark unzipped his black bag and pulled out a cross, a black book too skinny to be a Bible, and a bottle of water. From a pocket in his robe he pulled out a long, purple silk scarf. He put it across his shoulders so the ends hung down in front.

"Nikki," he said to her, "you take the book and hold it open for me. Mr. Bronski, hold up this crucifix."

"I'm not Catholic, sir," Bronski said.

"That's all right, if you don't have any objection," Father Mark said, and Bronski held up the cross.

Father Mark began reading from the book Nikki was holding, making crosses in the air. Then he opened the bottle and sprinkled water on the bus.

Did anyone else hear it groan? I thought. Father Mark circled the bus. With each sprinkle, the groans from the vehicle grew louder. After a minute the bus started to shake. It looked and sounded like a cornered animal trying to lash out at its attacker. Each drop of water provoked screams of what seemed like pain.

None of the others acted like they heard any of this, but I could tell that Father Mark felt something. By the time he'd circled the bus, his face was pale and his voice tight. Sweat rolled down his forehead. He had stopped reading from the book, but he was praying nevertheless, murmuring in what I guessed was Latin.

Finally he sighed, looked at Nikki and Bronski, and said, "We have to go inside the bus."

"We don't have a key," I said. But Notso stepped out, reached into his pocket, and produced a small, crooked piece of wire. You never know what to expect with Notso. It took him maybe twenty seconds to open the bus.

When the door opened, an indescribably putrid stench—like rotting meat—washed over us in hot waves. Bronski fell to one knee and started to retch. "Don't drop the crucifix!" Father Mark warned. I grabbed it just as Bronski lost his lunch.

"Lamar! Nikki! Follow me!" the priest commanded, and we climbed into . . . I'll call it *hell*. The stench, the heat, the sound of screaming—and the bus was swarming with flies of all kinds. Bluebottles, horseflies, and black flies buzzed and dived and bit.

Over it all, Father Mark shouted his prayers, throwing them out like punches, and sprinkled his holy water from the front of the bus to the back. As the battle got fiercer, my hand—the one with the cross in it—began to burn. I could see it getting red and blistered, but I held on as tightly as I could. Nikki tried to hold her book steady as tears ran down her cheeks. Flies clustered around her hair and eyes.

Father Mark thundered in English, "Begone! I command you in the name of all that is holy! Begone!" And I could feel something break. The bus stopped shaking, the screaming and the smell died away, and the flies streamed out the door and vanished into the cold air.

I put an arm around Nikki, who was crying softly. Father Mark leaned against a seat and tried to catch his breath. "Are you two all right?" he asked. We nodded slowly. "You guys requested a blessing," he said. "I didn't expect an exorcism."

"An exorcism?"

"Satan owned this bus," Father Mark

explained. "I don't know why. But we—well, the Lord—kicked him out. He can't work here anymore."

We thanked the priest and gave him back his stuff. Outside, Bronski was better. Notso just kept saying, "Man, I'm never going to say 'this stinks' about anything else again. That thing that happened when I opened the bus? *That* stinks."

Big, purple clouds were filling the sky by the time we were ready to leave, and the breeze was picking up. "There's a nor'easter coming," the priest said as we parted. "Did you hear?"

We hadn't. I dropped the others at their homes, and by the time I got to my place the wind was blowing hard, the temperature was dropping, and sleet was in the air.

I like storms. Not just because they cause school closings, like this one did. I like them because they're simple and powerful—just the same way they've been ever since the planet started. When there were no people, still somewhere there were blizzards and thunderstorms, the same way there were stars.

The nor'easter dropped about two feet of snow on Bridgewater. Power was out at my house for most of Friday—they usually start fixing things in town and then work their way out. When I looked out the front door on Friday afternoon, though, the world was peaceful and beautiful, glittering pure white in the sun. No one was going anywhere for a few days.

When I let Marcus out, he went crazy belly-surfing in the snow. After a while I walked out to shovel the drive. It's a long way—people ask why we don't have a snowblower— but I like the workout I get from shoveling snow.

By nightfall the power was back, and I called Dad at the hospital. He was starting to get a little restless, talking about getting back to work and all. "Dad," I said, making my voice deep like his, "you've got a gift here, and a burden. Your gift is a chance to relax; use it. Your burden is that you don't have a choice; live with it."

It made him laugh. "OK, Lamar," he said. "Those are wise words."

So I guess I was feeling good. Part of that was what had happened at the bus lot. I thought maybe Father Mark and the rest of us had really scared away Rumble's "wolves."

On Saturday morning I felt like taking a walk through the woods. Marcus was up for it, and the day was fresh and bright. We both had some work to do getting through the snow, but we knew the path by heart: down a steep hill into a wooded ravine, then along a creek bed for a mile or so till the path started going uphill. When we got to the top of the ridge, it was just a few hundred yards to the main road. We'd follow that back home.

The ridge had a fine view of the countryside. There was a little graveyard there that no one had taken care of for a long time. The five or six headstones were worn smooth, although you could read the date 1791 on one of them. Someone's birth or death, I didn't know which. As we passed the stones, I remembered it had been just three weeks ago that Miss Robin was buried.

"Thank you for remembering, Lamar."

She was sitting on one of the headstones, still wearing her white dress, seeming not to mind the cold. She studied me.

"So, you and Mr. Robert Emmett had a talk."

"Yes, ma'am. He wanted me to help him."

"Well, maybe you can, Lamar, maybe you can."

"He kept talking about wolves, Miss Robin. He said they were chasing him. In his dreams, anyway."

"Well, I told you about evil following him around. Someone like you, Lamar, you can probably see it."

"It looks like shadows."

Miss Robin smiled. *"Or mice, or flies."*

"But why is evil after him, Miss Robin? He doesn't seem like a bad man. He tried to rescue that girl, Penny. He risked his life."

"He lost his life, Lamar."

"But . . . he's here. He drives a bus. Dead people can't . . ."

"He's here because he has some work to do, Lamar. It's like this. When Mr. Emmett went over that cliff with Penny, what do you suppose he was thinking?"

"I don't know. I suppose he was scared."

"He was angry, Lamar, angry at himself. He believed the crash was his fault, that Penny's dying was all his fault. And the last thought that went through that poor man's brain was, 'If there's a hell, I deserve to go there.'"

"But he was wrong! He did what he could."

"That wasn't the way he saw it, Lamar. You see, when a person dies, if they are more or less peaceful, if they can say to themselves, 'I did what I could,' then they can pass on into peace. But if not, if they hate themselves or they think they've done something no one can forgive—that's called despair. And evil—it does exist, let me tell you—sniffs out despair and tries to own the soul of that person."

"But evil—the wolves—didn't get him."

"That's because of Penny. She knew that Mr. Emmett had tried to save her. And she used her wish to give him a second chance."

"Her wish?"

"When a good person dies, sometimes on their way to where they're going they get a chance to help someone they care about. It's a powerful chance, more powerful than life or death sometimes, especially for someone as innocent as a child, like Penny."

"She gave Mr. Emmett his life back?"

"A second chance, Lamar. He will die again someday. Everyone dies, you know. But he has some time to change. Time to accept himself, to forgive himself."

"But the wolves are still after him."

"Oh, yes. They feel cheated, and they'll try very hard to take him back before he can change. Meanwhile, they'll try to make him hate himself even more."

"Can't I just explain to him that he's not to blame?"

"Remember when you told him that Penny said thank you?"

"He said, 'She's got nothing to thank me for.'"

"Mr. Emmett has to find his own peace."

I told Miss Robin about blessing the bus, although she probably already knew. She smiled, nodded, and said, "Well, maybe you should've done that when I was driving. Maybe that old thing would have started easier in weather like this."

And then she was gone. I stood there for a minute, looking out from the ridge at the miles of white hills and black winter trees. *This world.* Then Marcus and I started home.

By Saturday afternoon I could hear the snowplows out on the main road. I played my DS, watched some hoops on TV. I phoned Dad, and we actually watched part of a game "together" while we talked. Later I whipped up some scrambled eggs and toast for supper. I was eating when I got a text from Nikki: *turn on channel 5.*

It was the news. A reporter was talking to a priest in a brown robe like Father Mark's.

". . . and we're all in shock here at St.

Philomena," the priest was saying. "He was extremely popular—well-loved by the students, the other faculty, and his brother Franciscans."

"And that's the story, Tom," the reporter said. "There's a real sense of sadness here at the tragic loss of this young priest. School officials say that grief counselors will be available for students coming to class on Monday, and school will be closed on Tuesday so that students and faculty can attend Father Mulroney's funeral."

Mulroney? I phoned Nikki. "That's Father Mark!"

"It's so awful, Lamar! I can't believe we just saw him, and now he's gone!"

"What happened?"

"It's so weird. Aunt Kate told me. Thursday night, when the weather was so bad, he got a phone call. The caller told the priests Father Mark lived with that an old nun was dying out at Precious Blood—it's a convent way out in the country. The caller said the nun was begging to see a priest, and Father Mark said he'd go. The other priests told him it was too dangerous to be out on the road, but he just said, 'Duty calls,' and started out."

"Did he make it?"

"Yes! That's the weird thing. When he got there no one was dying, and they said no one had called a priest."

"And?"

"What could he do? He got in his car and started back. On the way, while he was still out in the sticks, he saw a car in trouble on the side of the road. He pulled over to help. They needed a tire changed. While he was changing the tire, another car came speeding by and hit him. They say he was killed on the spot."

"Oh, man!"

"But whoever hit him didn't even stop. The people he was helping say it was a black car, but it was so dark they couldn't get a license number. The police are looking for a car with damage, but . . ."

"In that blizzard, the driver probably never saw him."

"That's not what the witnesses say, though. They said the car was going slow at first, like it was looking for something. When it got near, the driver put on the high beams, sped up, *and swerved toward Father Mark*! It's like they were trying to hit him!"

I started to get a really creepy feeling. "Nikki, you don't think this had anything to do with the bus, do you?"

Silence for a few seconds. Then, "I don't know what to think. I'm scared."

I spent a good part of Sunday at the hospital. Dad was walking around, excited about the balloon thing they were going to do on Monday. When I got home, I flipped on the news. "The police still have no leads on the hit-and-run accident that killed Father Mark Mulroney . . ."

On Monday I drove to school. I would have taken the bus, because later in the day I wanted to see if the blessing made any difference. But there was a chance I'd be bringing Dad home that day, so I needed the car.

So much for planning ahead. At lunch I got a call from Dad: they were running a couple more tests, and his procedure had been moved to Tuesday. After ballet, I wandered down to the foyer where the late-bus kids were gathered and saw Principal Weston addressing the group, a big grin on his face. A student from the computer center was videotaping him. I walked up next to Nikki, who gave me a look.

"As you all know," Weston was saying, "nothing is more important to Bridgewater High School than the safety and well-being of our students. That's why we've prevailed on Coastal Transportation to replace the old activity bus with a new, state-of-the-art vehicle. In addition to exceeding current emissions standards, this bus is equipped with high-tech security cameras. That way any incidents reported by passengers can be verified and appropriate action taken." At that point, the new bus pulled up outside the glass doors behind him.

There were *ooh*'s as we all moved outside to look. As I passed Weston he smirked at me and said, "Nice, eh Lamar?"

It wasn't a school bus. It was more like the kind of bus college sports teams travel in. Tall and long, with tinted windows. Seats with cloth upholstery and padded headrests. High in the adjustable driver's seat, a video screen and a microphone on his left, sat Rumble, looking kind of lost in his same old jacket and cap.

"Wow," I said to Nikki, "this is pretty cool."

"Maybe," she said, not smiling, "but it probably hasn't been blessed."

She was right about that. As the students crowded around the door, shreds of shadow mingled with them and flowed into the bus. Nikki was the last one on. I waved at Rumble and headed to the parking lot. I'd been in the car about ten minutes when my phone rang. It was Nikki, and it sounded like she was crying.

"What's the matter, Nik?" I asked.

"I don't know, Lamar! I'm just so . . . sad. Everyone on the bus is crying. I started thinking about Father Mark and . . . Why did that happen to him?" She started to sob. "Why do bad things happen to good people, Lamar? It just makes you feel like . . . like giving up!"

"Hold on, Nikki. Did you say the whole bus is crying?"

"It's just weird, Lamar. I don't think I've ever felt so . . . OH MY GOSH!"

"What?"

"The kids who just got off are screaming! I think we ran over someone!"

The bus ran over someone? *Who?*

"Nikki, where are you?" I asked, my voice louder than I meant it.

"We're at Notso's stop!" she said, gasping.

made a U-turn and drove toward Notso's
corner. I was two blocks away when I got
to the police cars blocking the scene. I parked
and ran to where the bus was. A bunch of kids
were standing around, including the late-bus
regulars. I was so glad to see that Notso was
among them. I could've hugged the guy.

"What the heck happened?" I asked.

"Dude tried to kill himself!" Notso said. "He
got off the bus, and when it started up again, he
jumped under the back wheels!"

"Is he dead?"

"No," Nikki said, "thanks to Notso and his friend. They dragged him out just when the tire bumped him."

"Yeah," Notso said, "but he was still really messed up. Crying, and like he was trying to get away so he could jump under the tires again!"

"I saw him crying on the bus," Nikki said. "Just like I was. It was like this gloom settled on everyone."

Bronski nodded. His eyes were red. "I couldn't believe how depressed I was getting. We were on the bus for just a few minutes, and I started thinking about all the saddest things that ever happened to me. I went from thinking about mistakes in chess to asking what's the point of anything? Why even bother living?"

"Are you guys OK now?" I asked.

They all said yes, that the sadness started to go away when the commotion started.

"Where's Rumble?" I asked. Then I saw him, sitting on the bottom step of the bus with his head in his hands. I walked over.

"Are you OK, Mr. Rumble?"

He looked up at me from bloodshot eyes and said, "I just about killed a kid. *Again.*"

"Is that what the police think?"

"No, they said I can go. But death keeps following me around, Lamar. I'm cursed!"

"It wasn't your fault. I'm sure of that," I said, but Rumble only shook his head.

There were several students still on the bus and at least ten more were standing around outside, wondering what they should do. The officer told Rumble not to worry, that the police would see that the kids got home. Rumble sighed, got into the empty bus, and drove off.

I dropped Bronski at his house and then drove Nikki to hers. No doubt, Principal Weston would soon hear about this.

A scare was all it turned out to be, luckily. Notso called that night to say his friend wasn't hurt, just confused. Even he couldn't figure out why he'd done what he'd done. Just like Nikki didn't understand why she'd started to cry.

And the late bus was still in business. Principal Weston came on the PA the next morning to announce that the new-and-improved bus would continue as scheduled, despite the previous day's "suspicious disturbance." Then he called four students, including Nikki, Notso, and me, to his office.

He was in a bad mood. "Can any of you tell me what happened last night?"

"I wasn't on the bus, sir," I said.

"Our security tapes show you at the scene, Lamar." I told him I'd stopped when I drove by the scene and recognized the bus.

"What happened on the bus, Miss Presley?"

"I'm not sure, Mr. Weston."

"Not sure?" He raised his voice. "I'll tell you why you're not sure. Because *nothing* happened on that bus! We have the tapes. Everything was perfectly normal until the . . . episode. Mr. Connor, how are you feeling this morning?"

I didn't know the kid with us, and I didn't know till later that he was the one who'd been hit. This morning he just stared at the floor. "I'm OK, sir."

"Well, if you begin to feel . . . upset, we have help here. I'd like you to go to Mr. Sprague's office and talk to him. In fact, I'll go down there with you in just a minute. Will you wait outside?"

When he left, Weston faced down Notso.

"Mr. Bright? You're absolutely sure that no one, uh, *suggested* to your friend that it would be amusing to frighten everyone by pretending to dive under the bus?"

"Tim wasn't faking," Notso said.

"If he were," Weston sneered, "it would be useful to have a friend who was in on the prank to 'save' him, don't you think?"

Notso stayed quiet.

"Well," Weston went on, "we have to think about the safety of all our students. As of this morning, all three of you are banned from the activity bus, do you understand? If you are staying after school, you'll have to find a ride elsewhere.

"And one more thing. Miss Presley, you will not write about this incident in the *Beacon*. I'm tired of your stories fanning the hysteria in the student body. Because that's what these pranks are creating—hysteria!"

He dismissed us. Back in the hall, we didn't have much to say. With Weston, you always got pretty much what you expected. Notso's friend Tim was there, waiting for the principal.

"I hope you guys aren't in trouble because

of me," he said. "I really don't know what happened. I just started to feel so bad, and for a minute there I really thought I wanted to die."

"It's OK," Nikki said to him. "You weren't the only one. There really is something going on with that bus."

At lunch I called Dad and found out they were going to keep him overnight after the balloon procedure, just to watch for complications. So I told Nikki and Notso I could take them home later.

Through the afternoon I thought about Rumble and what Miss Robin had told me about his needing to find his own peace. Judging from yesterday, he wasn't very close yet.

I was finishing up in the dance room when I saw Miss Robin again. It was for the last time, though I didn't know it then.

"Lamar."

"Yes, ma'am."

"I need you to do something for me."

"Sure, what is it?"

"You need to be on that bus with Mr. Emmett tonight."

I explained what Weston had said, but she waved it off. *"It's important for you to be there, Lamar. Mr. Emmett needs you."*

"Okay, ma'am, I'll try."

"Be brave, all right? You're a fine young man."

"Miss Robin . . . ?"

"Goodbye, honey."

When I met up with Nikki and Notso, I didn't know how to explain. I just said, "Sorry, I need to be on the late bus tonight."

They didn't question me even a little. "I'm with you," Notso said, and Nikki said, "Me too."

As we walked out of the school, the air felt clear and cold. Stars were already appearing, and the moon was almost full. The shadow on its face reminded me of a wolf.

Getting on the bus wasn't hard. No one was checking who was boarding. We were sure Weston would look at the security tape the next day, though. Detention was in our futures.

Rumble looked strange that night, kind of spaced out. I said hi to him and he didn't seem to notice. I turned to find a seat, and my mouth went dry.

The students in their seats were so covered in moving shadows that I couldn't make out their faces. "Do you see that?" I turned around to Notso.

"See what?" he said.

Things started getting strange when Rumble missed the first stop. He just drove right past it. When a couple of kids yelled, "Hey!" from the back, he stepped on the gas. By the time he'd blown by the second and third stops, we had to be doing sixty. I could hear cars honking, and the honking got louder when he blasted right through a red light on Water Street.

You'd think the police would have been on him right away, but they must have been busy at a crime scene or something. "Call 911!" I said to Nikki.

"My phone won't work!" she said. I could hear the same thing coming from some of the other seats. A couple of kids started to whimper just behind us.

I went up the aisle to see what could possibly be the matter with Rumble. He was hunched determinedly behind the wheel as the bus gained speed, and when he turned his scarred face to me, I saw what Miss Robin had meant by evil. Rumble's eyes looked like little points of red light. He grinned, and I saw long, canine fangs curling around either side of his mouth.

Before long we had left the city lights behind us. The bus careened along country roads. We had completely left our regular route. Rumble—or whoever had possessed him— seemed to be heading north.

I thought of trying to overpower Rumble— Notso would help me—and take the wheel. But it was too dangerous. Going off the road at that speed could be fatal.

It was so dark! Finally we whizzed by a sign I was able to read: Dunport, 20 miles. Where had I heard that name before?

I huddled with Nikki, Notso, and Bronski. It seemed like the four of us ought to be able to figure something out. "Maybe we're being kidnapped," Bronski said. "Maybe he's going to hold us for ransom."

"Either he's going somewhere, or we're going to run out of gas," Notso said. "These things don't get even ten miles to the gallon. Probably more like eight."

"Yeah," Bronski said, "but the tank holds thirty-five gallons."

"Wait," Nikki said, "he's slowing down."

She was right. But we were in the middle

of nowhere. As we slowed down, I looked out the window and saw, up ahead, a white cross planted by the roadside. In the moonlight I could see what looked like a cliff's edge and a huge blackness beyond. I knew instantly we were in Dunport—where Robert Emmett had died.

"Notso," I said, "he's going to stop. When he does, you need to get everyone off the bus. I'll distract him."

Sure enough, Rumble pulled over next to the cross. I went up to him. He sat sobbing quietly and looking out at the road.

"Mr. Rumble," I tried. "Robert."

He looked up at me, his eyes still glowing red in the dark. "You know what I have to do, don't you? The only way to stop the wolves is to give them what they want."

The engine idled, shaking the bus, while I tried to stall. Out of the corner of my eye I could see Notso fumbling with the emergency door in the back.

"That won't stop them! If you kill yourself now, they'll chase you forever!" I said to Rumble.

"Maybe that's what I deserve."

I felt a rush of cold air. The back door was open.

"You don't! Penny was grateful that you tried to save her! That's why you didn't die. She wanted you to have a chance to be at peace with yourself!"

I looked back and saw that the bus was empty now. At least the rest were safe. Then I saw that there was still one kid on the bus. Penny was coming toward me.

Rumble revved the engine and put his hand on the gearshift.

"Robert, wait!" I said. "Penny is here!"

He looked around, gave a desperate laugh, and slammed the bus in gear. The bus started to roll forward. Suddenly Penny grabbed my hand and nodded toward Rumble. I put my other hand on his shoulder.

I've never felt anything more powerful—and nothing sweeter—than the sensation that passed through me from Penny to Rumble. He stopped the bus and looked past me as if he was studying something far away. The red lights in his eyes went out, replaced by a silvery shining.

"Really?" he said. "Me?" He sighed deeply. His face relaxed into a smile, and his eyes closed. He slumped back in his seat. I knew he was dead.

I realized Penny was gone, too. And outside, blue lights were flashing—the police had found us. I walked to the back of the bus, climbed down into the cold night, and hugged Nikki and Notso and Bronski.

As I got out, several officers stormed the bus. I heard one of them yell, "Suspect down!"

Another officer walked up to me and said, "Are you Lamar Green?"

"Yes, sir," I said.

"I have a message. It's about your father. I'm supposed to get you to Bridgewater County Hospital as soon as possible."

We made to the hospital in about forty minutes. The information desk sent me to the ICU, and the doctor met me there by the nurses' station.

"Let's sit down," he said. "We did a balloon angioplasty on your dad this afternoon. In this procedure, we put a balloon in the arteries and inflate it. That squashes all the plaque, the stuff that's blocking the artery, against the walls. And when we deflate the balloon, the opening for the blood to pass through is wider."

"Is my dad alive?" I interrupted.

"Yes," the doctor said, "but he's very sick. In about one percent of these procedures, the balloon will cause a blood clot to loosen and travel to the brain. That can cause a stroke. I'm sorry . . . that's what happened to your dad."

"Can I see him?"

We went into the ICU. Lights were blinking and machines beeping and sighing. Dad was unconscious, an oxygen mask over his mouth. Even with the mask, I could tell that the right half of his face was sagging; it looked like it had started to melt.

"His face . . ."

"That's from the stroke," the doctor said. "I'm afraid the entire left side of his body is paralyzed as well. At least we think so. He hasn't regained consciousness since the stroke."

I don't know how you don't cry when stuff like this happens. At first I guess you're more shocked than anything.

"I'm sorry, Lamar," the doctor said. "Right now there's not much we can do until he comes out of the coma. You should probably . . ."

Suddenly the monitor next to my dad's bed

started screeching. Nurses and doctors rushed in and started shouting directions at each other.

The doctor just said, "It's your father's heart, Lamar. Please wait outside."

Twenty minutes later he came out. There was sweat on his forehead. "I'm so sorry, Lamar," he said. "There must have been another clot. Your father had a massive heart attack."

"Is he . . ." I couldn't say it.

"The machines are keeping him alive. But we're not sure he's going to regain consciousness."

They let me go back into the ICU and sit by him. I'd read that sometimes people in comas can really hear you, so I told him I loved him. I told him how much I wanted him to pull through, that he was my best friend. I had no idea how late it was. I think at some point I dozed off. And there was the dad I dreamed of. He and I were throwing the football around; he could always throw it hard enough to sting my hands. That's what he did in my dream. I laughed and went, "Ouch!" and he said, "Sorry, Lamar."

"Sorry, Lamar."

I snapped awake. Dad was looking at me and smiling. "Sorry to wake you up, son. You were looking so peaceful there."

"Dad?" I couldn't believe it. I hugged him the best I could. Just then a nurse came in. Her eyes got wide, and she hurried off. In two minutes the doctor was there. He looked completely shocked.

"Mr. Green," he said, "how do you feel?"

"Great," Dad said. "You were right about that procedure."

The doctor asked him to move his arms and legs, his fingers and toes, and to name the president. He shined a light into his eyes. Finally he shook his head and said, "I'm going to write a paper about this. Mr. Green, we'll move you to a regular room as soon as we can."

It was right after they moved him, by his bed in the ICU, that Rumble appeared. He was smiling, and Penny was holding his hand. He waved, and I read his lips as he faded away. "Thank you, Lamar."

Everything's fine in Bridgewater. Really . . .

Or is it?

Look for all the titles from the
Night Fall collection.

THE CLUB

Bored after school, Josh and his friends decide to try out an old board game. The group chuckles at Black Magic's promises of good fortune. But when their luck starts skyrocketing—and horror strikes their enemies—the game stops being funny. How can Josh stop what he's unleashed? Answers lie in an old diary—but ending the game may be deadlier than any curse.

THE COMBINATION

Dante only thinks about football. Miranda's worried about applying to college. Neither one wants to worry about a locker combination too. But they'll have to learn their combos fast—if they want to survive. Dante discovers that an insane architect designed St. Philomena High, and he's made the school into a doomsday machine. If too many kids miss their combinations, no one gets out alive.

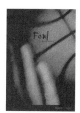

FOUL

Rhino is one of Bridgewater best basketball players—except when it comes to making free throws. It's not a big deal, until he begins receiving strange threats. If Rhino can't make his shots at the free throw line, someone will start hurting the people around him. Everyone's a suspect: a college recruiter, Rhino's jealous best friend, and the father Rhino never knew—who recently escaped from prison.

LAST DESSERTS

Ella loves to practice designs for the bakery she'll someday own. She's also one of the few people not to try the cookies and cakes made by a mysterious new baker. Soon the people who ate the baker's treats start acting oddly, and Ella wonders if the cookies are to blame. Can her baking skills help her save her best friend—and herself?

THE LATE BUS

Lamar takes the "late bus" home from school after practice each day. After the bus's beloved driver passes away, Lamar begins to see strange things—demonic figures, preparing to attack the bus. Soon he learns the demons are after Mr. Rumble, the freaky new bus driver. Can Lamar rescue his fellow passengers, or will Rumble's past come back to destroy them all?

LOCK-IN

The Fresh Start Lock-In was supposed to bring the students of Bridgewater closer together. Jackie didn't think it would work, but she didn't think she'd have to fight for her life, either. A group of outsider kids who like to play werewolf might not be playing anymore. Will Jackie and her brother escape Bridgewater High before morning? Or will a pack of crazed students take them down?

MESSAGES FROM BEYOND

Some guy named Ethan has been texting Cassie. He seems to know all about her—but she can't place him. Cassie thinks one of her friends is punking her. But she can't ignore how Ethan looks just like the guy in her nightmares. The search for Ethan draws her into a struggle for her life. Will Cassie be able to break free from her mysterious stalker?

THE PRANK

Pranks make Jordan nervous. But when a group of popular kids invite her along on a series of practical jokes, she doesn't turn them down. As the pranks begin to go horribly wrong, Jordan and her crush Charlie work to discover the cause of the accidents. Is the spirit of a prank victim who died twenty years earlier to blame? And can Jordan stop the final prank, or will the haunting continue?

THE PROTECTORS

Luke's life has never been "normal." His mother holds séances and his crazy stepfather works as Bridgewater's mortician. But living in a funeral home never bothered Luke—until his mom's accident. Then the bodies in the funeral home start delivering messages to him, and Luke is certain he's going nuts. When they start offering clues to his mother's death, he has no choice but to listen.

SKIN

It looks like a pizza exploded on Nick Barry's face. But a bad rash is the least of his problems. Something sinister is living underneath Nick's skin. Where did it come from? What does it want? With the help of a dead kid's diary, Nick slowly learns the answers. But there's still one question he must face: how do you destroy an evil that's inside you?

THAW

A storm caused a major power outage in Bridgewater. Now a project at the Institute for Cryogenic Experimentation is ruined, and the thawed-out bodies of twenty-seven federal inmates are missing. At first, Dani didn't think much of the news. Then her best friend Jake disappeared. To get him back, Dani must enter a dangerous alternate reality where a defrosted inmate is beginning to act like a god.

UNTHINKABLE

Omar Phillips is Bridgewater High's favorite local teen author. His Facebook fans can't wait for his next horror story. But lately Omar's imagination has turned against him. Horrifying visions of death and destruction come at him with wide-screen intensity. The only way to stop the visions is to write them down. Until they start coming true . . .

Southside High

Are you a SURVIVOR?

check out all the books in the

SURVIVING SOUTH SIDE

collection.

Bad Deal

Fish hates taking his ADHD meds. They help him concentrate, but they also make him feel weird. When a cute girl needs a boost to study for tests, Fish offers her a pill. Soon more kids want pills, and Fish likes the profits. To keep from running out, Fish finds a doctor who sells phony prescriptions. After the doctor is arrested, Fish decides to tell the truth. But will that cost him his friends?

Beaten

Paige is a cheerleader. Ty's a football star. They seem like the perfect couple. But when they have their first fight, Ty scares Paige with his anger. Then after losing a game, Ty goes ballistic and hits Paige. Ty is arrested for assault, but Paige still secretly meets up with him. What's worse—flinching every time your boyfriend gets angry, or being alone?

Benito Runs

Benito's father has been in Iraq for over a year. When he returns, Benito's family life is not the same. Dad suffers from PTSD—post-traumatic stress disorder—and yells constantly. Benito can't handle seeing his dad so crazy, so he decides to run away. Will Benny find a new life? Or will he learn how to deal with his dad—through good times and bad?

PLAN B

Lucy has her life planned: she'll graduate high school and join her boyfriend at college in Austin. She'll become a Spanish teacher and of course they'll get married. So there's no reason to wait to sleep together, right? They try to be careful, but Lucy gets pregnant. Lucy's plan is gone. How will she make the most difficult decision of her life?

RECRUITED

Kadeem is Southside High's star quarterback. College scouts are seeking him out. One recruiter even introduces him to a college cheerleader and gives him money to have a good time. But then officials start to investigate illegal recruiting. Will Kadeem decide to help their investigation, though it means the end of the good times? What will it do to his chances of playing in college?

SHATTERED STAR

Cassie is the best singer at Southside. She dreams of being famous. Cassie skips school to try out for a national talent competition. But her hopes sink when she sees the line. Then a talent agent shows up and tells Cassie she has "the look" he wants. Soon she is lying and missing glee club rehearsal to meet with him. And he's asking her for more each time. How far will Cassie go for her shot at fame?